The artwork for this book was hand drawn, dot by dot, using a crow quill pen and black drawing ink on 100 percent rag surface illustration board. The originals were drawn the same size as they are printed to ensure dot clarity, resembling grains of sand.

Photographs were used as reference for the drawings. A small model of the castle was built of foam core and polystyrene and photographed, along with a clay dragon and the two brothers who posed for Sir Christopher. The waves were those hitting the beach at Fort Baker near San Francisco.

The text of the book was set in 16 point ITC Novarese Book by Vulcan Typography Company. The book was printed by The Murray Printing Corporation on 80 pound Perkins and Squire Regular Offset paper. The book was bound by The Book Press, Inc.

He stood back and watched the waves break over the castle. Walls and battlements fell. The castle gradually disappeared. When only the towers remained, he put the toy in his bucket and turned to go. "Tomorrow I will build an even bigger castle," he said, and walked down the beach toward home.

"Saved just in time," said the boy, as he lifted the toy from the tower. Cold water splashed at his feet and about the castle as the rising tide moved across the beach.

"Help!" he screamed, but Sir Christopher was all alone on the top of the tower. The raging water kept rolling in, each wave bigger than the last. Storm clouds darkened the sky. Lightning crackled and thunder boomed. Suddenly, a hand reached down, snatching Sir Christopher into the air.

Giant waves leapt angrily at the tower, soaking Sir Christopher with icy water. He stood at the side, raised his hand, and cried again, "Stop! I am Sir Christopher, Builder of Castles, Tamer of Dragons, and Conqueror of the Black Knights. I order you to stop!" The ocean roared back with a deafening sound as another mighty wave crashed into the castle.

The water flooded the courtyard and poured into the rooms. Sir Christopher ran to the highest tower and began climbing. The water followed him up the spiral staircase. Sir Christopher turned and cried out, "I am Sir Christopher, Builder of Castles, Tamer of Dragons, and Conqueror of the Black Knights. I order you to stop!" The water continued to splash wildly at his feet and kept rising. Sir Christopher reached the top and stepped out onto the battlement.

"I am Sir Christopher, Builder of Castles, Tamer of Dragons, and Conqueror of the Black Knights," he called out. He watched as the ship vanished over the horizon. Sir Christopher, the castle defender, marched proudly up and down the beach.

Soon a cold wind began blowing and the waves grew larger and larger. He ran to the castle as huge waves rushed across the sand. The dragon let out a fearful cry, spread its wings, and flew into the air. The waves began pounding the castle walls just as Sir Christopher ran inside.

Before the Black Knights could reach the top of the wall, Sir Christopher called to the dragon. "Stop them," he ordered, and the dragon leaned its long neck over the battlement, roared out its thunder, and breathed a great cloud of smoke and fire. The Black Knights jumped from the ladders in terror, galloped their horses back to the ship, and quickly set sail. Sir Christopher ran down the stairs and out onto the beach.

Sir Christopher saw war horses and men in black armor ready for battle. From high atop the wall he shouted in his loudest voice, "I am Sir Christopher, Builder of Castles and Tamer of Dragons, and I command you to retreat." But the ship sailed right to the beach and dropped anchor. The men came crashing through the waves on their great horses. They set ladders against the walls and began climbing. Sir Christopher's castle was under seige.

Sir Christopher stood at an opening in the battlement and took a deep breath of the sea breeze. He looked down on the waves splashing the beach and then gazed out at the ocean. A speck appeared on the horizon—a ship sailing rapidly across the water. As it came closer, Sir Christopher could see it was the ship of the Black Knights. *And* it was heading straight for the castle.

Sir Christopher stood still and stared into the dragon's eyes. "Stop," he commanded. "I am Sir Christopher, Builder of Castles, and you are under my power." The castle suddenly grew quiet as the dragon stopped roaring and sat down. It swished its long, pointed tail as Sir Christopher announced triumphantly, "I am Sir Christopher, Builder of Castles and Tamer of Dragons!"

He turned to see a giant red dragon running up the stairs behind him. It flapped its leathery wings and made horrible scratching sounds with its long, sharp claws. Puffs of smoke came from its nose, and when it reached Sir Christopher it hissed and shot fire from its mouth. Sir Christopher ran to the top of the stairs. The dragon roared like thunder and followed.

"I am Sir Christopher, Builder of Castles!" he proclaimed. His words echoed about the courtyard and vanished over the high walls. Before him stood the many buildings that made up the castle. Turrets and towers pushed their way high into the clouds. Sir Christopher lowered the gates behind him. "Safe inside," he said, and began climbing the stairs. Halfway to the top, he was startled by a loud roar.

All morning he molded the wet sand. He built massive walls around an open courtyard with huge, round towers at each corner. Then he added battlements along the top of the walls and narrow windows facing the sea. He kept building until a fantastic castle stood on the beach. At last, he stood in front of the large, arched doorway and admired his creation.

T his is going to be the best castle ever," the boy said as he stood his toy on the beach. He filled his bucket with sand, poured it into a pile, and began to form a wall. "It will be a giant castle," he said, "with big, thick walls and great, tall towers." He filled his bucket again as the waves gently touched his feet.

FOR

LAUREN

Thank you, Ryan and Kevin

Macmillan Publishing Company
866 Third Avenue, New York, NY 10022
Collier Macmillan Canada, Inc.
First Edition.   Printed in the United States of America
10 9 8 7 6 5 4 3 2 1
Library of Congress Cataloging-in-Publication Data
Nolan, Dennis. The castle builder.
Summary: A young boy builds an unusual
sand castle on the beach.
[1. Sandcastles—Fiction. 2. Beaches—Fiction] I. Title.
PZ7.N678Cas  1987    [E]    86-23784
ISBN 0-02-768240-4

# THE CASTLE BUILDER

## STORY AND DRAWINGS BY DENNIS NOLAN

MACMILLAN PUBLISHING COMPANY   NEW YORK
COLLIER MACMILLAN PUBLISHERS   LONDON